THE CREEPY CLASSICS

CHILDREN'S COLLECTION

Dados Internacionais de Catalogação na Publicação (CIP) de acordo com ISBD

H691t	Hodgson, William Hope. The ghosts pirates / William Hope Hodgson. - Jandira, SP : W. Books, 2025. 120 p. ; 12,80cm x 19,80cm. - (Classics). ISBN: 978-65-5294-194-7 1. Literatura inglesa. 2. Clássicos. 3. Fantasia. 4. Imaginação. 5. Terror. 6. Suspense. I. Título. II. Série
2025-2530	CDD 823 CDU 821.111-31

Elaborada por Lucio Feitosa - CRB-8/8803
Índice para catálogo sistemático:
1 Literatura inglesa 823
2. Literatura inglesa 821.111-31

The Creepy Classics Collection
Text © Sweet Cherry Publishing Limited, 2024
Inside illustrations © Sweet Cherry Publishing Limited, 2024
Cover illustrations © Sweet Cherry Publishing Limited, 2024

Text based on the original story by William Hope Hodgson,
adapted by Gemma Barder
Illustrations by Nick Moffatt

© 2025 edition:
Ciranda Cultural Editora e Distribuidora Ltda.

1st edition in 2025
www.cirandacultural.com.br
No part of this publication may be reproduced, stored in a retrieval system, or transmitted in any form or by any means, electronic, mechanical, photocopying, recording, or otherwise, without written permission of the publisher.
This book is a work of fiction. Names, characters, places, and incidents are either the product of the author's imagination or are used fictitiously, and any resemblance to actual persons, living or dead, business establishments, events, or locales is entirely coincidental.

THE GHOST PIRATES

WILLIAM HOPE HODGSON

W. Books

JESSOP
A clever sailor

TAMMY
An apprentice sailor

THE FIRST MATE
The second in charge of the Mortzestus

The Captain
In charge of the Mortzestus

The Second Mate
The third in command of the Mortzestus

Williams
An older sailor who has sailed on the Mortzestus

Jaskett
The crew

Stubbins
The crew

Plummer
The crew

Chapter One

The Mortzestus stood proudly in the port at San Francisco. It was a large, sturdy ship, perfectly built for long voyages across the vast Atlantic Ocean.

I was excited to have been given the chance to work aboard the Mortzestus as part of its crew. It would be the largest ship I had ever worked on, and the furthest I had ever sailed. Despite my enthusiasm, as I left the shipping office and headed over to the ship with my belongings in a sack on my back, I became aware of strange looks coming from other sailors.

'Hey, you there!' an older sailor called out, hurrying to catch up with me. 'Heading to the Mortzestus?'

I nodded.

The old sailor whistled through his gapped teeth and shook his head. 'You're a braver man than I,' he said. 'Wouldn't be caught within twenty feet o'that thing. You do know it's cursed, don't you? It's got bad luck seeping out of its wood. A ship like that is unprotected from bad spirits!'

I looked at the man, certain that he was playing a joke on me. 'Cursed?' I said, laughing. 'Nonsense.'

The old man shrugged and walked away. 'You can't say you weren't warned!' he called back over his shoulder.

Climbing up the gangplank, the Mortzestus looked strong and powerful. Its ropes were neatly wound, and the sails were clean without a single patch. The Second Mate checked off my name as I stepped aboard. 'Jessop. Good, you will be part of my watch,' he said. 'We tend to do the night shifts, I'm afraid.'

'I've no problem with that, sir,' I said, tipping my hat.

As I found my bunk below deck, I introduced myself to the rest of the crew. They were all as excited and cheerful as I was to be on the Mortzestus. We were all new to the ship, including the Captain, First Mate and Second Mate, apart from one crew member. Williams.

'Tell me, Williams,' I said, as the boat pushed out to sea. 'Why was I warned about this ship?'

Williams rubbed his chin thoughtfully. 'Too many shadows,' he said. 'Men get frightened off.'

'Shadows?'

But Williams refused to explain any further. Instead he shrugged his shoulders and turned away. 'Whatever they are, they're not going to stop me from getting paid.'

***

Our first day at sea was calm, bright and clear. I tried to sleep, knowing that my first night watch was coming up, but the sounds of my crewmates working above my head kept me awake.

'Shake your boots, lad,' said Jaskett, an older sailor with bright red hair, as we were put in charge of the ship's wheel. He breathed in the night air and gazed up at the thousands of stars in the sky. 'If every journey out to sea were as calm as this, I'd bring my grandmother along!' he said.

I laughed and was about to reply when I saw a shadowy

figure appear suddenly behind him. The strange figure walked slowly towards us, in a curious lopsided way.

'Who's that?' I asked, thinking it might be a sleepwalker from the day watch.

'Who, lad?' he asked, looking at me oddly. 'There's no one there.'

Chapter Two

The shadowy figure disappeared as suddenly as it had come into sight. I blinked and rubbed my eyes.

'Don't worry,' Jaskett said, kindly. 'The first few night shifts can be tough. Your mind can play tricks on you.'

I wanted to believe him, and yet I was certain that was not the case. The figure had been there as sure as Jaskett was standing in front of me now.

The following night, I got out on deck earlier than the rest of my watch. I searched the part of the deck where I had spotted the figure the night before, but nothing was there except the gentle lapping of the ocean against the ship's hull.

I had been tasked with looking after one of the ship's apprentices – a young man called Tammy. It was his first voyage, and he was eager to learn all he could about the sea.

apprentice
Someone who works for somebody else to learn their skill or trade.

At around 3 a.m. the ship's bell rang out to say that all was well on board. As the ringing trailed off into the distance, I heard a voice in the air. 'Jessop,' it whispered.

I whipped my head around, and looked at Tammy to see if he was playing a trick on me. But the young lad was standing as still as a statue. His eyes round and wide, staring at something. It was the figure again. The very same one that I had seen the previous night.

'You see it too?' I asked.

Tammy nodded, too frightened to speak.

I passed the wheel over to him and raised my lantern. When the light was thrown over the figure, he slunk backwards, swiftly climbing over the side of the ship.

'Where did he go?' I asked.

'Jessop! What are you doing?' shouted the Second Mate, marching towards me. 'Can you explain to me why, exactly, the apprentice is holding the ship's wheel?'

18

'Sir, there was a–' Tammy began.

'It was nothing, sir,' I interrupted, knowing that the Second Mate would not take kindly to stories of strange figures appearing and disappearing. 'I just wanted to give the lad a try at the helm. I'll take the wheel back now, Tammy.'

The Second Mate looked suspiciously at us both. Tammy stayed silent, though I could see his hand was trembling.

Chapter Three

Tammy did not speak a word about the figure to anyone. He quietly got on with his work. Occasionally I would catch him staring at the spot where the figure had sloped back into the sea, but it was not until a few nights later that Tammy finally mentioned it.

We had just secured the main sail in place and had set about sweeping the deck, when the

Second Mate began shouting at someone, or something, at the top of the mast.

'You there! What are you doing?' he called. 'Come down at once!'

'What is it, sir?' I asked, following the Second Mate's eyeline.

'That man, there!' he said. 'He's disobeying my orders. I told everyone to come down!'

At first, I could not see anyone. The night was cloudy, and the moonlight was dim.

'Th–there!' cried a quiet, stuttering voice. It was Tammy, standing by the side of the Second

Mate, pointing just as he had a few nights before. 'It's the same figure. I'm sure of it!'

'Plummer! Stubbins! Get up there and bring that sailor down,' the Second Mate commanded. Two young sailors dropped what they were doing and began to climb the rigging. They were quick and made it to the lookout in no time.

'There's no one up here, sir,' called Plummer.

'What are you talking about?' demanded the Second Mate. 'He's right there!'

It was then that I, too, saw the man the Second Mate was talking about. It was the same, lopsided, shadowy figure I had seen twice already. My blood ran cold, and I instantly looked at the trembling Tammy.

'It's all right,' I said calmly, and told the boy to go below deck. 'Sir, I see him too, but I am not certain everyone can,' I said quietly to the Second Mate.

'Don't be absurd,' the Second Mate snapped at me. 'There is an unaccounted man on this ship, he is there as plain as ...' He stopped suddenly and his eyes darted about the ship. 'Where did he go?' he asked, looking from me to the lookout. 'He was right there!'

'I know, sir,' I said, nodding, 'I have seen him, too.

The Second Mate's face turned

scarlet. Whether it was out of fear, anger or embarrassment I could not tell you.

'Plummer, Stubbins, get down here this minute!' he shouted. 'We will carry out a search of the ship for stowaways.'

The crew searched every inch of the ship, from the Captain's quarters to the top of the mast. Every person was accounted for, and no one was missing.

stowaway
A person who hides on a boat, train, etc. to travel without being seen.

quarters
Rooms or lodgings given to specific people.

As the first watch took over, I wandered through our sleeping quarters to find Williams.

'May I speak with you? I asked, ducking my head to perch on the end of his narrow bunk. Williams nodded, swinging his legs out and sitting up. 'You talked about shadows when we first met. I think I might have seen them.'

Williams stared at me, a determined look in his eye. 'It's happening again,' he said, wearily. 'But the owners

of the Mortzestus pay well and I need the money. No shadows are going to chase me from this ship. Not now. Not ever.'

With that, Williams lay back down in his bunk and turned away from me.

Chapter Four

Each night, the First Mate, Captain and Second Mate met up on deck to switch over from the day watch to the night watch. They discussed what had happened during the day, and what might happen overnight. Mainly, these conversations focussed on the weather, or repairs for the ship, or crew members who were sick or misbehaving. This night, however, I overheard the First Mate and the

Captain's rolling laughter, and I moved to the stairway that led up to the deck to hear them.

'You've been listening to too many stories, my good man!' said the Captain, chuckling. 'People are jealous of the Mortzestus's strength and size. They'll say all sorts of things!'

'Maybe you've been sleeping on the job?' teased the First Mate.

I heard the Second Mate move a few steps away and take a few deep breaths. To be accused of dozing on the night watch was one of the most insulting things you could say to a sailor.

'It was neither of those things,' said the Second Mate, trying to control his anger. 'But we will leave it for now as I can see I am only amusing you. Have we had a weather report?'

'Calm, not a breath of wind,' said the First Mate. 'You'll be in for a quiet night, unless any of your *friends* come to visit, of course!'

The laughter ebbed away as the

First Mate and Captain headed to their own quarters.

***

The night was just as they had predicted; calm and quiet. I was tasked with tidying up the deck when I saw one of the top sails had come loose. There was very little wind, so it flapped limply, the loose ropes dangling free.

'Sir, a sail has come loose. Shall I climb up and fix it?' I asked.

The Second Mate scowled. 'No, the sailor responsible should do it,' he said. 'Who secured the top sail?' he shouted.

'That was me, sir,' replied Plummer.

'Well, you didn't do a very good job. It is loose.'

Plummer looked up at the sail, confusion covering his face. 'But sir, I swear I tied it up tight,' he said.

The Second Mate was in no mood to be argued with. He watched as Plummer climbed the rigging and set to work securing the sail once more. Then, an extraordinary thing happened. A gust of wind came out of nowhere

Instead of falling straight on to the deck, Plummer managed to grab on to the rigging, but he was not quick enough to save himself completely. He fell with a hard bump on to the wooden deck and knocked himself out.

***

'Sir, I am telling you the truth,' exclaimed the Second Mate to the Captain. They were standing by Plummer's bunk

as the sailor slept fitfully. I tried not to listen in, but our quarters were not exactly spacious, and every sailor could hear what was being said.

'There was no wind last night,' said the Captain. 'This man is clearly unfit for the work!'

'But he is a fine sailor, sir,' said the Second Mate. 'I assure you, it was as strong a wind as I ever felt.'

At that moment, Plummer stirred. After a drink of water and an assessment of his bumped head by the ship's doctor, the Captain asked him for a full report on what took place.

'Well, sir, it was the wind,' Plummer said, rubbing the spot on his head where he fell. 'A strong, strange, powerful wind.'

Chapter Five

For a few days, all was calm and settled on the ship. No one mentioned the strange wind, and Plummer got on with his work as though nothing had happened.

The memory of the strange figure I had seen on the deck was still preying on my mind. The Second Mate was convinced there was a stowaway somewhere on board, but what I saw did not look like a runaway. In fact, it did not look human at all.

I tried to speak to Williams again one night when we were working together up on deck.

'Leave it alone!' he said, grumpily. 'I just want to get through this voyage without any more trouble.'

'I only wish I knew what I had seen,' I replied. 'I can't get the image out of my head.'

Williams glared at me, but before he had a chance to answer, we were both distracted by another loose sail. The same one that had come loose when Plummer had fallen off the mast.

'I'll go up,' Williams said, sighing, as he started to climb the rigging. 'Fetch me some extra rope so I can secure it.'

'I'm not sure you should,' I tried to warn him. 'You saw what happened to Plummer.'

Williams ignored me and continued to climb. I ran off to

find the extra rope and almost collided with the Second Mate. 'Goodness, Jessop, slow down!' he said. 'Where are you off to in such a hurry?'

'It's Williams, sir,' I said, panic beginning to rise up in me. 'He's climbing the rigging. The sail has come loose again. The same one that …'

Before I could finish my sentence, the Second Mate pushed past me. 'Get down here at once!' he shouted up at Williams.

I fetched the rope and hurried back to where the Second Mate was standing, staring up at Williams. The wind had started to pick up again, and I saw a flicker of fear on the Second Mate's face as he reached up to keep his hat from blowing off his head. 'Williams, I said come down!'

'He can't hear you, sir,' I said, as the wind grew stronger. The loose sail whipped angrily from side to side, like a fish out of water. Williams held on to the mast with one hand and grasped fruitlessly with the other.

'Williams!' the Second Mate bellowed louder. 'This is your commanding officer! I demand that you …'

In that moment, time slowed down. I watched in horror as Williams's foot slipped off the mast, the sail hitting him with such a force that he was thrown

into the air. His legs and arms flailed desperately as he hurtled towards the deck below.

Chapter Six

Williams's death made the crew nervous. One of our watch was dead and we were all shocked and upset. Talk of the ship being cursed began to be whispered across our watch's bunks as we tried to sleep.

After a long night shift, I was put in charge of the ship's wheel. The sun was coming up bright and strong, and I was grateful for the warmth of it on my tired

face. I had not slept well since
Williams had died.

As I looked out to sea, I saw
a shimmer across the water.
At first, I thought it was simply
a reflection of the sunrise, but a
strange haze seemed to lift itself
out of the ocean. It was grey
and dense, like a London fog
in autumn. The dark cloud grew
in size so that it was as large as
the Mortzestus itself and hovered
over the ship before covering
it completely.

Then, in a moment, it was gone.

'What was that?' Tammy gasped, appearing at my side.

'I don't know,' I replied. 'I haven't seen anything like it before ... wait, what is that?' I stepped away from the wheel and stared off the side of the boat. A ship had appeared

no more than one hundred yards away. 'Do you see it?' I asked Tammy. But before the young apprentice could answer, our own ship's wheel began to spin wildly. I leapt forward to grab it, and by the time I looked out again, the other ship had disappeared.

Tammy's eyes were wide with fear as he looked from me to the ocean.

'You saw it, didn't you?' I breathed. But Tammy stayed silent as he heard the familiar heavy tread of the Second Mate approaching.

'Can you tell me why the ship is facing in completely the wrong direction?' the Second Mate shouted at me. 'It's clearly been a long night and you have been sleeping on the job.'

I stood up straight, insulted to be on the receiving end of such an unjust accusation. 'No, sir, not at all!' I said, fiercely. But the Second Mate pushed me aside to take the wheel for himself.

'Go back to your bunk and get some rest,' he commanded. 'You are on lookout tonight, and I can't have you falling asleep up there.'

I knew there was little point in arguing. So, I nodded and left, ignoring the stares of my shipmates as I headed below deck.

Chapter Seven

Strange dreams invaded my sleep, and I woke in a cold sweat. I heard Plummer and Stubbins complaining with old Jaskett as they put on their work clothes to get ready for night watch.

'The ship is cursed, I'm telling you,' said Stubbins, pulling on his work boots.

'I've worked on hundreds of ships,' said Jaskett. 'This one's the strangest of them all.'

I dressed quickly and climbed the rigging to take my post on the lookout. The night was clear and cold. Thousands of stars lit up the sky and for a moment I felt at peace. I tried to picture the Mortzestus successfully docking in England, but the image was clouded with thoughts of poor Williams, the grey figures and the strange vanishing ship.

As I rubbed my hands together to keep warm, I caught a glimpse of a green light blinking in the distance. I took out my telescope and saw a ship heading towards us. I rang the lookout bell.

'What is it, Jessop?' called the Second Mate.

'A ship, sir, off the port side!' I called back.

The Second Mate drew his own telescope out of his pocket and inspected the ocean. 'Nothing there, lad!' he called, sounding confused.

I looked again and saw that the ship had disappeared. It could not have changed course in so short a time, and it could not have sunk, either. It had simply vanished.

Moments later, the green light flickered again, and the ship reappeared, closer this time.

'There, sir!' I said, gesturing wildly, but by the time the Second Mate had marched over to look, the ship had once again vanished.

'Jessop, get down here!' the Second Mate commanded. 'Clearly you need your eyes examined. Jaskett, take over.'

I climbed down the rigging and passed the telescope over to Jaskett who shrugged in apology.

'Now, Jessop, I know the past week has been a little unsettling,' the Second Mate began, sternly. 'But you need to pull yourself together or I'll have you mopping the deck until we dock in England.'

He was suddenly interrupted by the lookout bell.

'Ship, sir!' called Jaskett. 'Ship approaching on the port side!'

The Second
Mate sighed with
frustration as he
pulled out his telescope
once more. 'Blast it, Jaskett!'
he cried. 'Not you, too! There is
nothing there, I tell you!'

I looked out at the inky, black
ocean. The Second Mate was
right. There was nothing there.
And yet, from the lookout,
Jaskett and I had both seen a
ship. Something very strange
was happening. I could see from
the Second Mate's expression
that he was starting to believe

that something wasn't right. He turned to me, confusion and fear spreading over his face.

'What is happening, Jessop?' he asked.

But I could not answer.

Chapter Eight

The Second Mate called us out of our bunks early the next night. The usually smart officer looked tired. His hair was not combed, and his jacket was not fully buttoned.

'Now men, this evening I would like you all to …' he paused.

'Help me,' cried a faint voice.

My shipmates and I looked at each other.

'Who said that?' asked the

Second Mate, staring wildly at each of us.

'Help me!' The voice came again. It was louder this time and seemed to be coming from the far end of the ship. Instinctively we ran towards it. As we reached the end of the ship, we saw something quite unbelievable.

Jaskett appeared to be in the middle of a fight, but there was no one else in sight. Blood trickled from his nose and his shirt had been badly torn – yet he was quite alone. He was swinging his arms in the air fists clenched, as though trying to punch some invisible opponent.

'Jaskett, stop this at once!' said the Second Mate, too scared to approach the fighting man.

Jaskett fell to the floor, as though he had been pushed by whatever invisible force was attacking him. Stubbins flew to Jaskett's side and dragged him away.

'It's all right, old fella,' said Stubbins. 'You're all right now.'

Jaskett looked up at his young shipmate, dazed. 'It was there. The figure. I chased him thinking it was the stowaway.' Jaskett breathed heavily. 'But this was no human, this was … something not of this world.'

'Take him below deck,' the Second Mate ordered, kindly. My shipmates and I watched as Stubbins helped Jaskett up to his feet and supported him under his arm as they walked away. Silence fell. Only the creaking of the ship and the slight breeze in the sails could be heard.

The Second Mate paced up and down, shaking his head. 'Right, gentlemen,' he said, stopping to regain his composure. 'Listen carefully to your instructions for tonight's watch.'

As we paid attention to the Second Mate, we could feel the ship rock under our feet. The wind picked up slightly and raindrops scattered over the wooden deck.

'Jessop, I want you to …' the Second Mate stopped talking.

A bright bolt of lightning split the sky as the rain turned into heavy, weeping droplets. 'Wake the day watch immediately!' he shouted. 'Tell them a storm's incoming. All hands on deck!'

The wind and rain hit my face as I ran to the day watch's quarters. Some of the men were in their bunks, and some of them had heard the thunder and were already throwing on their clothes.

'All hands on deck!' I shouted. 'Right now!'

Chapter Nine

The storm raged, growing steadily stronger and stronger. Even with both watches, the Captain, First and Second Mate on deck, the boat still swayed violently from side to side. Sails flapped viciously in the wind as I tried to make my way across the deck, slipping on the seawater and rain.

Suddenly, shouts and screams filled the air, even louder than the thunder in the sky above us.

I stopped what I was doing and stared. A group of men had climbed the rigging to secure the sails and they were now all trying to get down at once, scrambling over each other as though being chased by unseen demons. I blinked away the rain, trying to take in the scene. It was like nothing I had seen before.

Lightning cracked and lit up the air, and I swore for a moment I saw an unearthly figure standing on the mast. The storm did not trouble him a bit – he moved with the boat as though he were part of it. He threw back his head and laughed at the screaming men. As the lightning faded, so did the image of the figure.

I spotted Plummer among the men who had scrambled down the mast and ran to help him up. His clothes were as torn and ragged as if they had been clawed and ravaged by a tiger.

'What is it?' I gasped. 'What has happened?'

'Stubbins,' he gasped, struggling for breath. 'Stubbins did not make it down.'

Horrified, I looked from Plummer up to the mast and saw that Stubbins was still desperately clinging to it. His eyes were tight shut, frozen in fear.

'Stubbins!' I shouted as loudly as I could manage. It was useless. He could not hear me over the noise of the storm.

I took a deep breath, ready to shout again, when the ship suddenly lurched. A huge wave crashed on to the deck, sweeping everyone off their feet. When we recovered, I frantically searched the mast with my eyes, but

Stubbins was no longer there.

'Man overboard!' I shouted, trying to raise the alarm that Stubbins had been lost out at sea. Only Plummer and Tammy heard me above the chaos. The three of us ran wildly from one side of the ship to the other, searching the

night-time waters and calling for Stubbins. But there was no sign of him. He was gone.

Plummer sank to his knees, tears mingling with the rain and seawater. I clutched young Tammy, sorry that an apprentice should witness so much horror on his first ever voyage.

I busied myself the best I could with practical tasks. I swept water overboard and took my turn at the wheel when others got tired. I refused to look up, in case the horrible laughing figure was still watching us all scurry around in panic. I spotted the First and Second Mate on the front of the ship. Their heads were bent together and, although I could not hear what they were saying, they looked to be disagreeing.

When the rain stopped, the storm drifted, the ship settled and the sun finally rose, the crew huddled in hushed groups on the deck.

Some said they were resting or drying themselves in the daylight, but we all knew why we were really there. We were terrified. Another of our shipmates had

died in frightful circumstances
and there was no longer any point
in denying that something evil
had taken over the ship.

Chapter Ten

I decided to check on Jaskett. I had not had time to see him since his fall. As I moved through our quarters, I tried to make sense of what had happened. But there was no explanation for the events since the Mortzestus had set sail. When I reached Jaskett's bunk, I saw that it was empty and the mattress stripped. The ship's doctor was nearby. I grabbed his arm. 'Where is Jaskett?' I asked.

The doctor looked worn out. He sighed heavily and looked down. 'He did not make it,' he said, gently. 'He died while everyone was on deck during the storm.'

The news almost made me give up hope. Three men who had set sail with us from San Francisco, hopeful for a safe crossing, were now gone. Williams, Stubbins and now Jaskett. I went back to my bunk and sat down heavily. Every single one of my muscles ached with unbearable tiredness, and yet I could not sleep. I stared at the wooden beams above my bunk, my mind racing.

'Jessop?' Tammy whispered. 'Are you awake?' I put my head out of my bunk and looked along the length of my quarters to see the young boy doing the same. He swung himself out of his bunk

and made his way to the small, upturned barrel at the end of our quarters that we used as a table. I slowly got up and joined him. A deck of cards was scattered all over the floor. No one had the energy to pick them up.

'Tell me what is happening, Jessop. Please!' Tammy begged.

'I wish I could,' I replied. I paused for a moment. 'That is, I do not know, for certain.' Something had been stirring in my mind, and I wondered whether Tammy was the right person to tell it to.

Tammy grabbed my hand. 'But you think you have an idea?' he asked. 'Please tell me.'

I sighed and looked about to see if anyone else was listening. 'I believe this ship is somehow unprotected,' I began. 'Perhaps it was not blessed when it took its first voyage, or perhaps it has received some bad luck at some time, but I think bad spirits are able to board the Mortzestus.'

Tammy's whole body was trembling. 'And the evil spirits have been making all the terrible things happen?' he asked.

'I don't know. Perhaps I am talking nonsense,' I said, suddenly unsure I should be saying anything at all. Would it make things worse to speak my thoughts out loud? 'It was just something someone said to me back in San Francisco. I can't get it out of my head.' How I wished I had listened to that old sailor back at the port.

Tammy jumped up and pulled at my arm. 'You need to tell the Captain!' he said. 'We need to head to the nearest dry land and get off this ship as fast as we can!'

I patted his hand. It was trembling more than ever. 'It's okay,' I said, soothingly. 'It will all be okay.'

But I could not be sure if things would ever truly be okay again.

Chapter Eleven

'Jessop? What are you doing here? You should be sleeping,' the Captain said, surprised to see me in his private quarters. He was stooped over his desk, closely studying maps and charts. The darkness under his eyes made it seem as though he had not rested since the storm. Tammy stood behind me in the doorway, too nervous to step inside.

'Forgive me, sir,' I replied.

'I wanted to talk to you, if you have a moment?'

The Captain sighed and beckoned for me to take a seat. Tammy finally followed me in, carefully shutting the door behind us.

'What is it, Jessop? I am very busy. That blasted storm knocked us off course and I am trying to figure out how to get us back on it again.'

'That is what I am here about, sir,' I began. 'For weeks now, I have witnessed strange things happening on the night watch. Ghostly figures of men who should not be there. Otherworldly mists that surround the ship. Terrible winds that appear out of nowhere. Then last night …'

The Captain held out his hand for me to stop talking. 'You do not need to tell me about last night,' he sighed. 'I *should* tell you both that this is all nonsense. Silly stories get thrown around after too many days at sea.' The Captain got up from his desk and started to pace. He stopped and studied my face. 'You are a clever lad, Jessop. I believe you have taken your Mates' training?'

I could feel Tammy staring at me. I had told no one but the Second Mate that I had recently passed my training to become a Mate myself. I did not want the other men to see me as any different from themselves. But perhaps it was a good thing that the Captain knew – he may have taken me more seriously because of it.

'Yes, sir,' I replied. 'I think the ship is unprotected from bad spirits. I know it sounds like a tale from a child's storybook, but the more I see, the more I am convinced.'

To my amazement, the Captain nodded in agreement. Sighing again, he sat down and leant forward. 'When I took this job, the Mortzestus was the only ship available,' he said. 'It seemed madness to me that such a fine ship had not already been taken, so

I snapped her up. When news got out that I was to captain the ship, I started getting letters warning me that she was cursed. I am ashamed to say I ignored them. I thought the other Captains were jealous that I had command of such a fine vessel. I now see I was wrong.'

I did not know whether to be happy or frightened that the Captain believed my story. 'What are we to do?' I asked.

The Captain stood up and started pacing once more. 'We carry on, boy,' he said. 'The sooner we port, the sooner we can get off this cursed ship and get back to some kind of normality. At night, we will strap lanterns around the deck to throw light on to every corner and force these bad spirits away. It is the only way to beat them.'

My heart sank. I was not sure what I was expecting the Captain to say, but I knew that lanterns alone were not going to help the Mortzestus, nor any of the men aboard her.

Chapter Twelve

When I went on deck to begin my watch the next evening, I saw that it was flooded with light. The day watch had strapped lanterns to every available surface. They burnt so bright it almost looked like daylight. The glow warmed me for a moment or two, before I saw the Captain, First and Second Mate approaching.

'Jessop, I have informed the Mates of your theory,' said the Captain.

I could see the Second Mate glaring at me. He was no doubt angry at me for going over his head to speak to the Captain, but I refused to look at him. This was no time for ego.

'We are agreed that you should not inform any of the other men about what you think,' the Captain added.

'Why not, sir?' I asked. 'They have seen horrible things too. Surely they deserve to know what is happening?'

'Do you want a mutiny on your hands, boy?' the Second Mate said, angrily. 'What we need now is to sail this ship to England as quickly as we can. Then we can all forget we ever had the misfortune to lay eyes on her.'

mutiny
Openly disobeying or fighting against the leaders in charge.

Perhaps the officers were right, but a big part of me felt uncomfortable about keeping my shipmates in the dark. I knew I had no choice but to obey my superiors. The night passed without any unfortunate events, and everyone agreed it must have been the lanterns that kept the evil spirits at bay. The sun rose and we made our way back to our quarters.

Before going below deck, I threw my arm around Tammy's shoulders. 'How are you?' I asked.

The boy shrugged, but before he could answer, I saw something begin to rise out of the ocean. It was the same grey, foggy mist that we had seen before. It rose in a large cloud and settled on the water. Tammy and I leant over the side to get a better look and saw something so awful; it chilled us to the very pits of our stomachs.

Beneath the water were the dark, unmistakeable outlines of four huge ships. Impossibly, they passed beneath us like giant whales, dark and menacing. 'Are they ... ships?' Tammy said, almost unable to get out the words.

'Yes,' I said. 'I believe they are.'

We could not take our eyes off the ghostly figures before us. My mind could not help but wander to the crews who must have once sailed them upon the ocean. I started to tremble as I realised something so terrible, I could hardly admit it. The haunting, grey figures who had been causing such terror on our ship must once have been the crew of those great vessels now at the bottom of the ocean. Their spirits angry at having been lost at sea, were now seeking their revenge on any unprotected ship or sailors who dared pass their final resting place.

'Come along you two, our watch is over,' said the Second Mate.

I could do nothing but point at the water, unable to speak. The officer paled as he took in the sunken ships. 'I must speak to the Captain,' he cried. 'Get inside, at once!'

Chapter Thirteen

When Tammy and I stepped down into our quarters, we saw that the bunks which should have been full of sleeping sailors were completely empty.

'Lanterns cannot keep us safe for long!' Plummer's voice echoed through the space. He and the rest of the watch were crammed into the small seating area at the end of our quarters. Men were standing, arms folded, listening to Plummer talk. 'The Captain and the Mates know far more than they are letting on. It's not right.'

A grumble of agreement rippled through the men.

'So, what are we going to do?' asked a young sailor. 'We can hardly jump ship and swim for it!'

The men murmured amongst themselves.

'We take charge!' said Plummer, punching the air with his fist. 'We need to look out for ourselves before any more of us end

up the same way as Jaskett, or Williams or …' Plummer stopped as Stubbins's name caught in his throat and his eyes filled with tears. He coughed, before continuing. 'It ends tonight!'

'Wait!' I said quickly, walking into the circle of men. 'We are in the middle of the Atlantic Ocean. Who among us can navigate their way to England without the Captain?'

'You could!' blurted Tammy. 'You've taken your Mate's training. If anyone here can lead us, it's you! I don't trust the Captain or

the Mates, Jessop. They're going to steer us to certain doom!'

I placed my hands on Tammy's shoulders. 'Calm yourself,' I said. 'We need to work together if we are going to survive this voyage. We need to have faith in our commanding officers, not mutiny against them.'

Silence fell among the watch. The men looked at Plummer, waiting for him to speak.

'Very well,' he said, grudgingly. 'But if our situation does not improve soon, we will take action no matter what.'

As the day watch busied themselves above our heads, I tried to sleep. I watched Tammy's bunk until I could be sure that he was resting, then I said a silent prayer to keep watch over the Morzestus. In truth, I had no idea whether we would reach England, or if more of us would suffer. As I finally closed my eyes, I did not have a clue what was to face us that very night.

Chapter Fourteen

I woke to the sound of my shipmates getting ready for the night watch. Not a single man spoke as they pulled on their boots and oilskin coats. Plummer stared at me as we climbed up the steps on to deck. 'We are trusting you, Jessop,' he hissed.

'It is not *me* you need to trust,' I replied, as calmly as I could. 'I have no more control over dark forces than you do.'

Plummer simply shook his head and made his way over to the Second Mate to receive his duties for the night ahead.

'Gather round, men!' the Second Mate called. 'This evening will be a little different to usual.' I could see that he looked tired. His hands shook as he spoke and so he folded his arms to try and hide the trembling. 'We are turning the ship in,' he announced.

The men looked at each other in wonder. This had never

happened to any of them before. To turn a ship in means to stop sailing. To let the ship float safely until it is ready again. The sails would be taken down and, most importantly, it would only need a few men to stay on deck.

'The Captain believes this will be the safest thing to do until whatever plagues this ship has moved on.'

I noticed Plummer was smiling and I was relieved that his mutinous thoughts had passed.

'I need a couple of volunteers to stay on deck and help me,' said the Second Mate.

I stepped forward. I had already seen so much, and I knew far more than most of my watch. 'I'll do it,' I said. I felt Tammy beside me.

'Me too!' he said.

I turned to him quickly. 'No, Tammy,' I said, firmly. 'I appreciate the support, but I can do this by myself.'

Tammy looked hurt. 'The truth is, I feel safer with you than by myself,' he said.

I sighed and nodded.

'Very well.'

The Second Mate clapped his hands. 'As Tammy and Jessop have volunteered, the rest of you can go back below deck.'

I watched, as the very same men who had only hours earlier been plotting to overthrow the Captain, happily disappeared back into the safety of our quarters. I smiled a little bitterly and braced myself for the long night ahead. The Second Mate took the wheel to keep the ship steady, while I climbed the rigging to sit in the lookout.

The night set in and the hours passed slowly. The sky was as black as it had been all voyage, with the moon only a thin fingernail of light in the sky.
I dreamt of a warm, safe bed on dry land, with fresh food and water, rather than the dried stale bread biscuits we ate on board.

I had slipped so far into my imagination that at first I did not see the sinister grey fog emerge from the ocean once again. When I did, I saw that it was ten times as big and wide as it had been before. I quickly rang the lookout

bell and called out: 'Sir! Sir!'

The Second Mate ran to the side of the ship and stared in terror. The eerie fog hovered ever closer until it was floating over the ship like a low-hanging dark cloud. Then, the most impossible thing happened. If I had not seen it with my own eyes, I would not have believed it. The cloud dissolved into hundreds of human forms, in the shape of ghost pirates.

Chapter Fifteen

I jumped from the lookout and climbed down the rigging as fast as I could, my eyes darting about the deck for Tammy, as the horrible beings swarmed all over the ship.

'All hands on deck!' I shouted. 'All hands on deck!'

As I reached the bottom of the rigging, I saw the doors to our quarters burst open and the men of the night and day watches flood on to the deck. As they stopped and stared in disbelief, the ghostly pirates fell upon them, and they started to battle. The air was filled with the crew's cries and shouts of anger and pain.

Just then, I spotted Tammy hiding behind the anchor wheel. 'They have come for us!' he whimpered, terrified.

'I must go and help,' I said. 'Stay here and be quiet. Do not let them see you.'

If I could go back in time and change the decision to leave Tammy alone, I would. It is something I have regretted ever since. As I rushed to join the fight, I heard a scream that suddenly choked off into silence.

'Tammy!' I shouted, knowing immediately that the awful sound belonged to him. But when I got to the wheel, it was deserted. Tammy was gone. I never saw him again.

Just then, the ship lurched violently from side to side. My shipmates and I rolled helplessly across the deck, unable to keep our footing as the pirates laughed, easily staying upright.

The ship was taking on water from both sides and, with one final frightful lurch to the right, she capsized. I was lucky that I was already standing close to the edge of the ship so was not dragged under as the Mortzestus sank.

My heart was pounding, and my body ached from the freezing water. If I were to die here, I might be damned to join the crew of phantom pirates. The prospect made me more determined to live than ever. It was then that I saw a familiar green light. It was the same ship I had seen many nights earlier.

I prayed and prayed that this was no ghostly figure and that it would not disappear again as I swam as hard as I could towards it.

'A ship! Men! This way!' I shouted. I looked around hoping to see my shipmates swimming as fast as they could behind me. But to my despair, the sea was empty. The Mortzestus had sunk to the inky blackness beneath, and my crew had joined her there.

    So, I swam. With all the strength I had left. That is when you found me.

Chapter Sixteen

I am the Third Mate of the Sangier, the ship that picked Jessop up on that fateful night. Jessop has asked me to write a note at the back of his story to tell you that everything he has said is true, as far as I can witness.

A few weeks ago, we came

across the Mortzestus. We knew the ship and where it was heading, but it was miles off course. Our Captain made the decision to sail as close as we could to inform the crew that they were heading in the wrong direction. As we got closer, we saw Jessop in the lookout and signalled to him with a green light. He seemed to notice us, but a few moments later, it seemed as though they could no longer

see us. We signalled twice more, and nothing happened. After hours of trying, we decided to move on.

Then, last night we saw the Mortzestus again. We could see fighting on deck and hundreds of pirates battling with the crew, though strangely there was no pirate ship anywhere to be seen. We sailed closer, but sadly not in time to save the ship. We watched it lurch from side to side, though there was only a slight breeze in the air. No one on the Sangier could understand what made the Mortzestus rock so violently. We saw it capsize and the pirates vanish, along with the crew.

We continued to sail towards the shipwreck and found only one survivor. Jessop.

I, the Mates and Captain of the Sangier, will now sign this as a true account of the Mortzestus.

AUTHOR ⚓ BIOGRAPHY
WILLIAM HOPE HODGSON

William Hope Hodgson was born in Essex in 1877. At the age of thirteen, he ran away from school and became a cabin boy in the Merchant Marines. During his time at sea, Hodgson had many adventures including rescuing a man from shark-infested waters. But he was also bullied by older sailors. These experiences unfolded in his writing, and his horror and fantasy tales often explore revenge.